Goat and Donkey and the Noise Downstairs

For Viv again, and Davey too! – S.P.
For Molly and Helen – R.J.

OXFORD
UNIVERSITY PRESS
Great Clarendon Street, Oxford OX2 6DP

Oxford University Press is a department of the University of Oxford.
It furthers the University's objective of excellence in research, scholarship,
and education by publishing worldwide in

Oxford New York
Auckland Cape Town Dar es Salaam Hong Kong Karachi
Kuala Lumpur Madrid Melbourne Mexico City Nairobi
New Delhi Shanghai Taipei Toronto

With offices in
Argentina Austria Brazil Chile Czech Republic France Greece
Guatemala Hungary Italy Japan Poland Portugal Singapore
South Korea Switzerland Thailand Turkey Ukraine Vietnam

Oxford is a registered trade mark of Oxford University Press
in the UK and in certain other countries

British Library Cataloguing in Publication Data available

ISBN: 978-0-19-272817-3 (Hardback)
ISBN: 978-0-19-272818-0 (Paperback)

10 9 8 7 6 5 4 3 2 1

Printed in China

Paper used in the production of this book is a natural,
recyclable product made from wood grown in sustainable forests.
The manufacturing process conforms to the environmental
regulations of the country of origin.

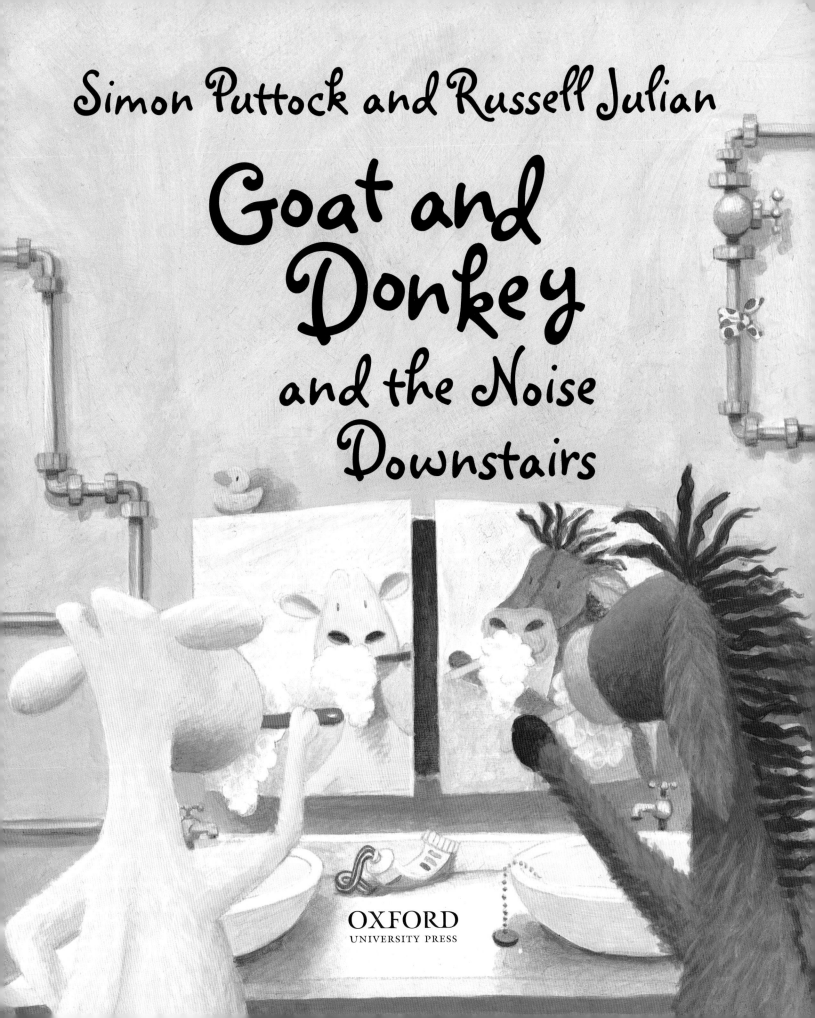

Simon Puttock and Russell Julian

Goat and Donkey

and the Noise
Downstairs

OXFORD
UNIVERSITY PRESS

Goat woke up one night and it was dark, and there was a NOISE DOWNSTAIRS! 'Oooh!' said Goat, feeling trembly all over. 'I do not like noises downstairs in the night. It might be burglars!'

Goat wished very hard that Donkey was there to make him feel safe.

But, he thought, if I call out, the BURGLARS
might hear and come and FIND me!
Oh dear, oh dear, oh dear! Whatever shall I do?

'I know,' said Goat. 'I will pull the covers right up over my ears, and perhaps the burglars will go away.'

But from underneath the covers,
Goat heard ANOTHER noise!

Oh no! thought Goat. The burglars have NOT
gone away! Whatever shall I do now?
'I know,' said Goat. 'I will creep into Donkey's room
and wake him up. Donkey ALWAYS knows what to do.'

Goat crept
out onto
the landing.

CLANG!

There was
ANOTHER
noise
downstairs.

Goat stopped
creeping and
DASHED into
Donkey's room.

'Donkey,' he whispered.
But Donkey did not stir.

Goat gave the bed a shake.
But still Donkey did not stir.

Goat reached out to nudge Donkey awake.

But Donkey WASN'T THERE! Just Donkey's dear old Rabbity where Donkey was supposed to be.

On no! thought Goat. The burglars have stolen Donkey! All at once Goat felt sad. Then he felt frightened. And THEN he felt very cross indeed with the burglars for stealing Donkey.

Goat knew what he must do next.
He must be BRAVE.
He must go downstairs and rescue
Donkey before the burglars got away!

Goat grabbed Rabbity to shake at the burglars.
Rabbity wasn't very fierce, but he would have to do.
'Right,' said Goat. 'I am ready to be brave!'

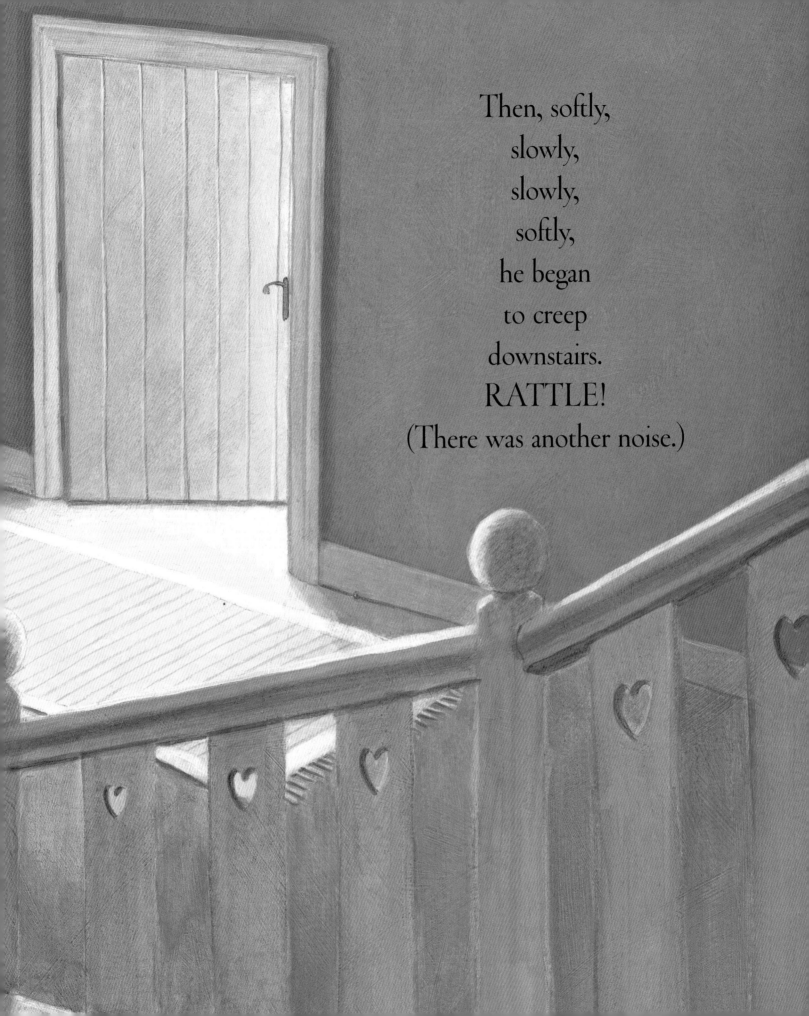

Then, softly,
slowly,
slowly,
softly,
he began
to creep
downstairs.
RATTLE!
(There was another noise.)

Goat nearly jumped out of his skin.
The noise had come from the kitchen!
Oh dear! Goat did not like being brave,
but he knew he must.

Slowly,
softly,
softly,
slowly,
Goat crept
up to the
kitchen door.
He reached
for the handle and . . .
CLUNK!
(Yet ANOTHER noise.)

Goat gasped. The hairs all over him stood up on end!
'It's now or never,' he whispered to himself,
and he BURST into the kitchen.
'You FIENDS!' cried Goat, bravely brandishing Rabbity.

'Just
you
give
me
back
my
best
friend
Donkey!'

But there was not a gang of great big burglars in the kitchen – not even a couple of very SMALL burglars.

Sitting at the kitchen table was
ONE surprised Donkey,
having a late-night snack!

'But I'm right here,' said Donkey,
'having a little late-night snack.'
'Oh, Donkey!' cried Goat, feeling very foolish.
'I've been so worried and so scared!'
And he burst into tears.

'There, there,' said Donkey.
'Take a deep breath and tell me all about it.'

Goat sniffed hard and told
Donkey all about the imaginary
burglars and a stolen best friend.

'Oh, Goat,' said Donkey.
'Sometimes you are the
muddliest person I know.
But you are also very,
VERY brave.'

'Am I?' asked Goat.
'Yes,' said Donkey.
'In that case,' said Goat, looking longingly
at Donkey's snack, 'I think being brave
makes me very, very HUNGRY.
Can I have a snack, too?'

'I think,' said Donkey, 'that a very, VERY brave
Goat deserves a great big midnight feast!
Let's rustle one up right now.'
'Oh goody,' said Goat, feeling better already.
'Yes, let's.'

And that is exactly what they did.